Disney · PIXAR
Cars 2

Adapted by **Lisa Marsoli**

Illustrated by **Caroline LaVelle Egan, Andrew Phillipson, Scott Tilley, and Seung Beom Kim**

A GOLDEN BOOK · NEW YORK

Materials and characters from the movie *Cars 2*. Copyright © 2011 Disney/Pixar.

Disney/Pixar elements © Disney/Pixar, not including underlying vehicles owned by third parties; and, if applicable: Pacer and Gremlin are trademarks of Chrysler LLC; Jeep® and the Jeep® grille design are registered trademarks of Chrysler LLC; Maserati logos and model designations are trademarks of Maserati S.p.A. and are used under license; Mercury is a registered trademark of Ford Motor Company; Porsche is a trademark of Porsche; Sarge's rank insignia design used with the approval of the U.S. Army; Volkswagen trademarks, design patents and copyrights are used with the approval of the owner, Volkswagen AG; Bentley is a trademark of Bentley Motors Limited; FIAT and Topolino are trademarks of FIAT S.p.A.; Corvette, El Dorado, and Chevrolet Impala are trademarks of General Motors. Background inspired by the Cadillac Ranch by Ant Farm (Lord, Michels and Marquez) © 1974.
Published in the United States by Golden Books, an imprint of Random House Children's Books, a division of Random House, Inc., and in Canada by Random House of Canada Limited, Toronto. Golden Books, A Golden Book, A Big Golden Book, the G colophon, and the distinctive gold spine are registered trademarks of Random House, Inc.

ISBN: 978-0-7364-2780-7
www.randomhouse.com/kids
Printed in the United States of America
10 9 8 7 6 5 4 3 2 1

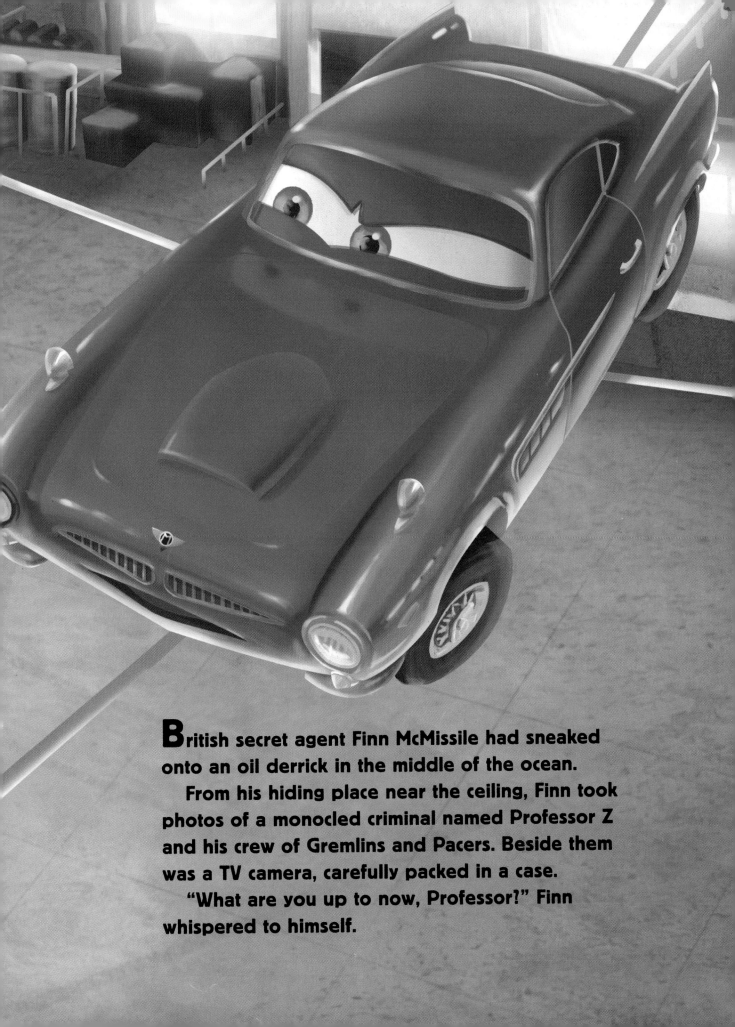

British secret agent Finn McMissile had sneaked onto an oil derrick in the middle of the ocean.

From his hiding place near the ceiling, Finn took photos of a monocled criminal named Professor Z and his crew of Gremlins and Pacers. Beside them was a TV camera, carefully packed in a case.

"What are you up to now, Professor?" Finn whispered to himself.

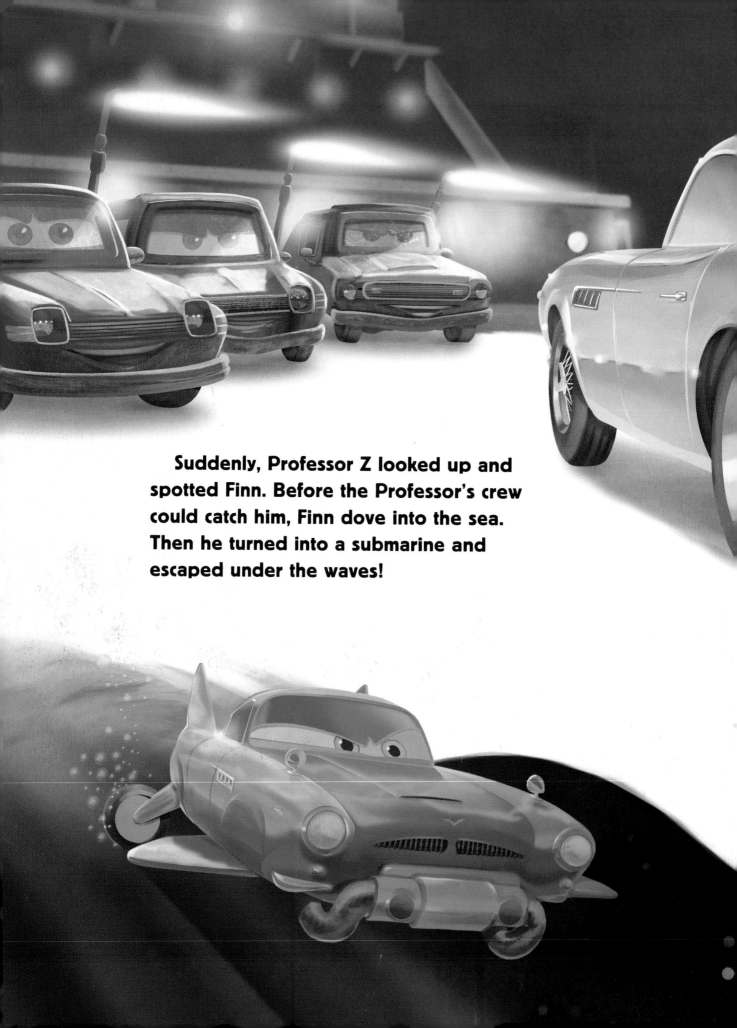

Suddenly, Professor Z looked up and spotted Finn. Before the Professor's crew could catch him, Finn dove into the sea. Then he turned into a submarine and escaped under the waves!

Far away in Radiator Springs, Mater the tow truck couldn't wait for his best friend, Lightning McQueen, to return home. Lightning had been away at a race for weeks, and Mater really missed him.

When Lightning arrived home, he and all his friends celebrated at the Wheel Well restaurant. Former oil tycoon Miles Axlerod was on TV. To introduce his new alternative fuel called Allinol, Axlerod was hosting the World Grand Prix—a series of three races to be held around the world.

A famous Italian race car named Francesco Bernoulli was also on the TV show. Francesco bragged that he was faster than Lightning McQueen. Lightning agreed to enter the World Grand Prix to prove him wrong!

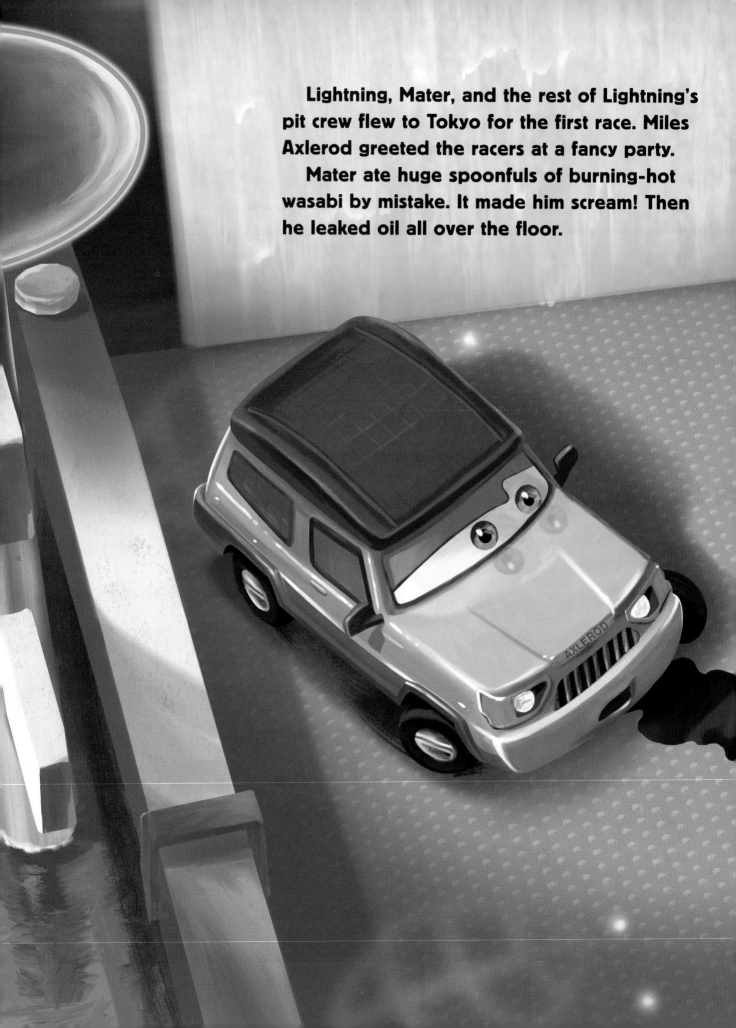

Lightning, Mater, and the rest of Lightning's pit crew flew to Tokyo for the first race. Miles Axlerod greeted the racers at a fancy party. Mater ate huge spoonfuls of burning-hot wasabi by mistake. It made him scream! Then he leaked oil all over the floor.

"You have to get ahold of yourself!" scolded Lightning. "You're making a scene!"

Mater went to the bathroom to clean up. There were so many confusing buttons in the stall, he didn't know which one to push!

Just then, an American secret agent, Rod "Torque"
Redline, rolled into the bathroom. Professor Z's goons
Grem and Acer followed Torque in and attacked him!
Suddenly, Mater flung open his stall door, knocking Grem
aside. During the commotion, Torque secretly attached a
small device to Mater.

Finn McMissile and his fellow agent
Holley Shiftwell were at the party to
retrieve some information from Torque.

When Mater came out of the
bathroom, Holley thought *he* was
the American secret agent she and
Finn were supposed to meet! She
told Mater to look for her at the
first World Grand Prix race.

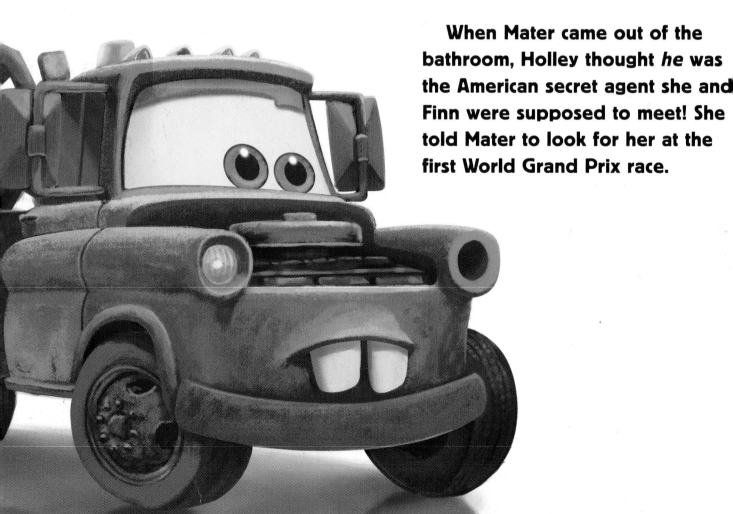

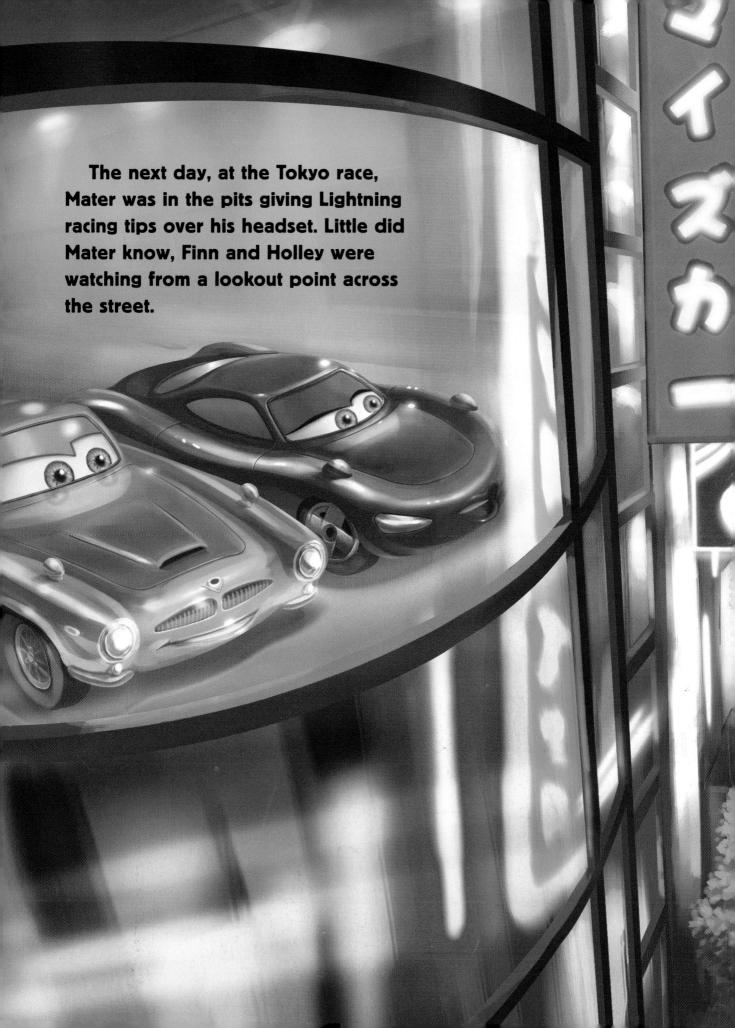

The next day, at the Tokyo race, Mater was in the pits giving Lightning racing tips over his headset. Little did Mater know, Finn and Holley were watching from a lookout point across the street.

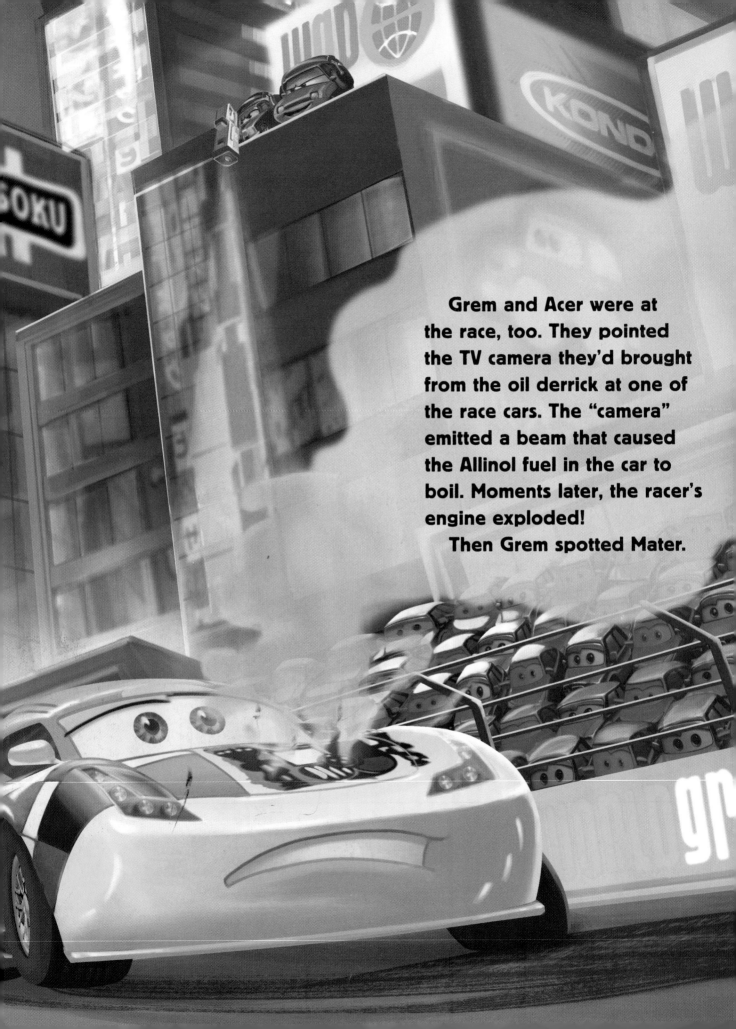

Grem and Acer were at the race, too. They pointed the TV camera they'd brought from the oil derrick at one of the race cars. The "camera" emitted a beam that caused the Allinol fuel in the car to boil. Moments later, the racer's engine exploded!

Then Grem spotted Mater.

Grem, Acer, and the rest of Professor Z's gang prepared to attack the tow truck. They were determined to get the device that Torque had planted on Mater. Holley warned Mater through his headset.

"Get out of the pit now!" she told him.

Shortly after, the Gremlins
and Pacers started closing in
on Mater. Finn bravely rushed
in and fought them off.
    Mater thought it was a
karate demonstration! He
cheered for Finn.

Lightning thought Mater was giving him instructions on his headset. Lightning was so confused, he began swerving all over the racetrack. Francesco had the opening he needed—and won the race!

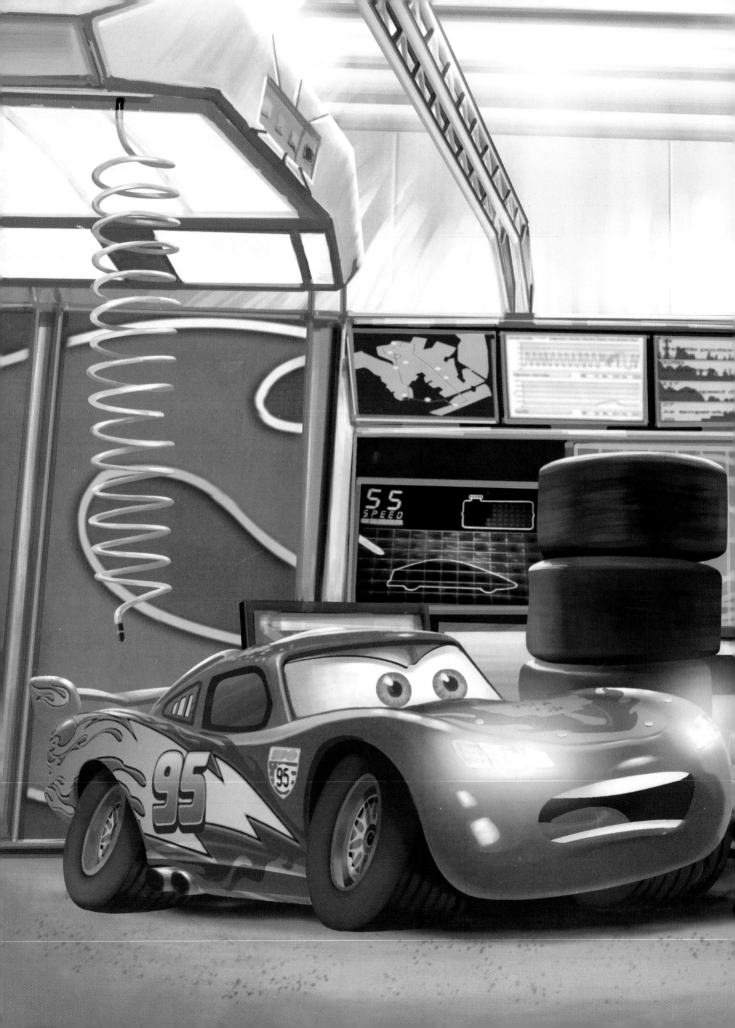

When Mater made it back to the stadium, he was sad to discover that Lightning had lost. Mater tried to explain what had happened, but Lightning didn't believe him.

"I lost the race because of you!" Lightning yelled angrily.

Mater felt terrible. He headed to the airport to go home.

An airport security car pulled the tow truck aside, then revealed his true identity: Finn McMissile! Finn warned Mater that he was in danger.

Grem and Acer soon found Finn
and Mater and began chasing them!
Finn hooked himself to Mater and
fought off the goons.

Suddenly, Holley arrived in a spy
plane. Finn and Mater made it up
the ramp just in time!

Back at the hotel in Tokyo,
Lightning read a farewell note
from Mater.

Lightning was sad. "I didn't
really want him to leave," he said.

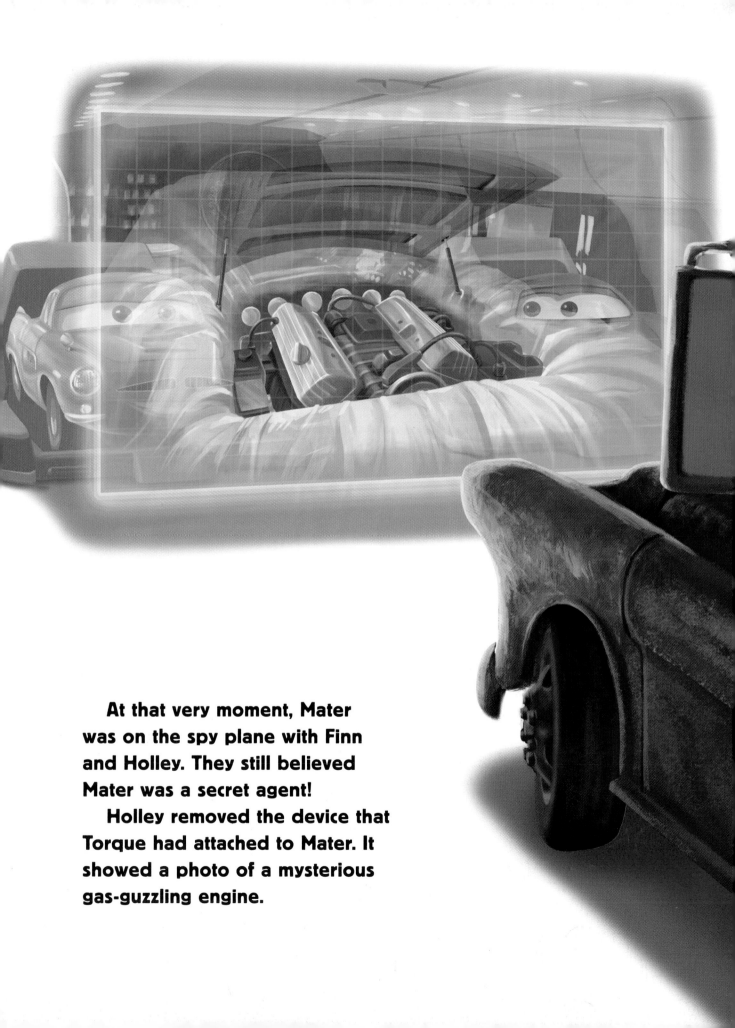

At that very moment, Mater was on the spy plane with Finn and Holley. They still believed Mater was a secret agent!

Holley removed the device that Torque had attached to Mater. It showed a photo of a mysterious gas-guzzling engine.

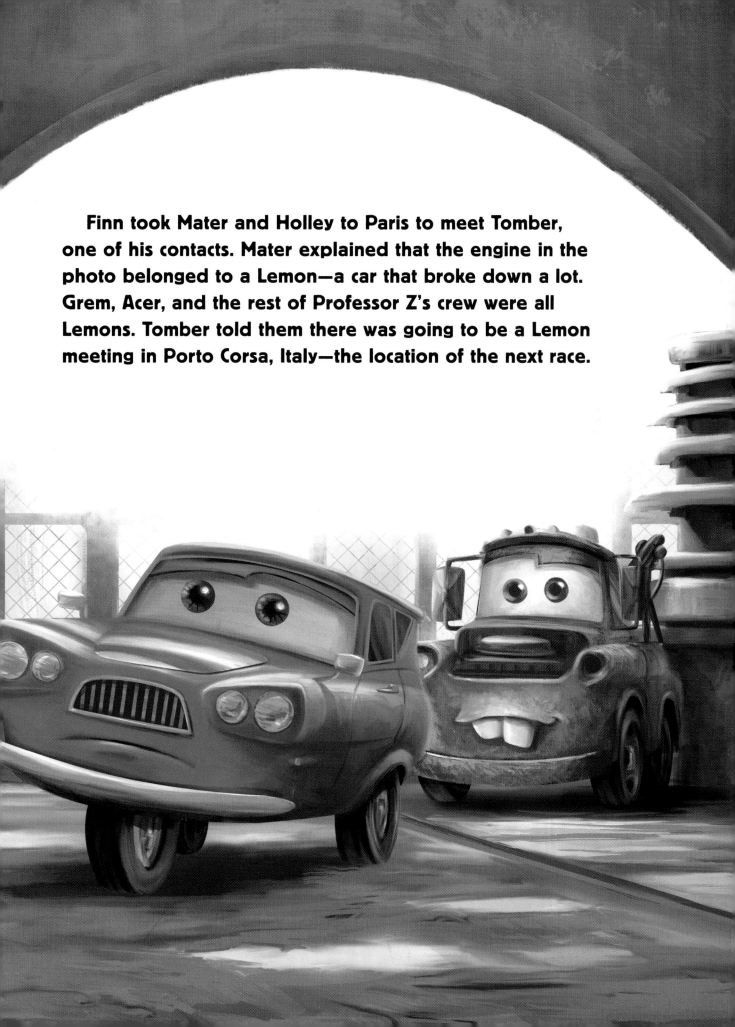

Finn took Mater and Holley to Paris to meet Tomber, one of his contacts. Mater explained that the engine in the photo belonged to a Lemon—a car that broke down a lot. Grem, Acer, and the rest of Professor Z's crew were all Lemons. Tomber told them there was going to be a Lemon meeting in Porto Corsa, Italy—the location of the next race.

Lightning and his friends were already in Italy for the race. They visited Luigi and Guido's hometown. Luigi's wise Uncle Topolino talked to Lightning about Mater. "Everybody fights now and then, especially best friends," said Uncle Topolino. "But you gotta make up fast."

Meanwhile, Finn, Holley, and Mater were on a spy train heading to the Lemon meeting in Porto Corsa. Holley projected a hologram onto Mater to disguise him as one of the Lemons' tow trucks so he could sneak into the meeting. Holley also gave Mater some cool spy gadgets!

In his disguise, Mater drove into the casino where the Lemon meeting was being held. Holley and Finn were outside, listening to everything through Mater's headset.

Professor Z introduced the Lemons to their mysterious "Big Boss," who appeared on a TV screen. Only his engine could be seen—the same engine that was in Torque's photo! The Big Boss was the mastermind of the evil plot involving Allinol and the exploding race cars. He promised to bring wealth and power to Lemons everywhere!

Finn and Holley figured out what was going on. The Lemons were blowing up cars to make it look as if the alternative fuel, Allinol, was unsafe. The second World Grand Prix race was already under way. Finn had to stop the Lemons before they hurt the race cars. But a helicopter captured him with a giant magnet!

With Finn out of the way, Grem and Acer aimed the fake camera at the race cars as they zoomed down the Porto Corsa racetrack. Seconds later, Shu Todoroki, the racer from Japan, suffered an engine blowout! As he lost control, he crashed into several other racers.

At the finish line, Lightning shot past Francesco Bernoulli. "That's what I'm talking about! *Ka-chow!*" yelled Lightning.

In an interview after the race, Miles Axlerod admitted that Allinol might be responsible for the exploding race cars. But Lightning insisted that he would still use Allinol for the last race in London. "My friend Fillmore says the fuel is safe. That's good enough for me," he said.

The Big Boss heard this and gave the Lemons a new order: Destroy Lightning!

At that moment, Mater's disguise malfunctioned and disappeared. But before the Lemons could catch him, he escaped, using his spy gadgets!

Mater parachuted to the Porto Corsa racetrack. He wanted to warn Lightning that his life was in danger. But the Lemons dragged Mater away before he had the chance to talk to his friend.

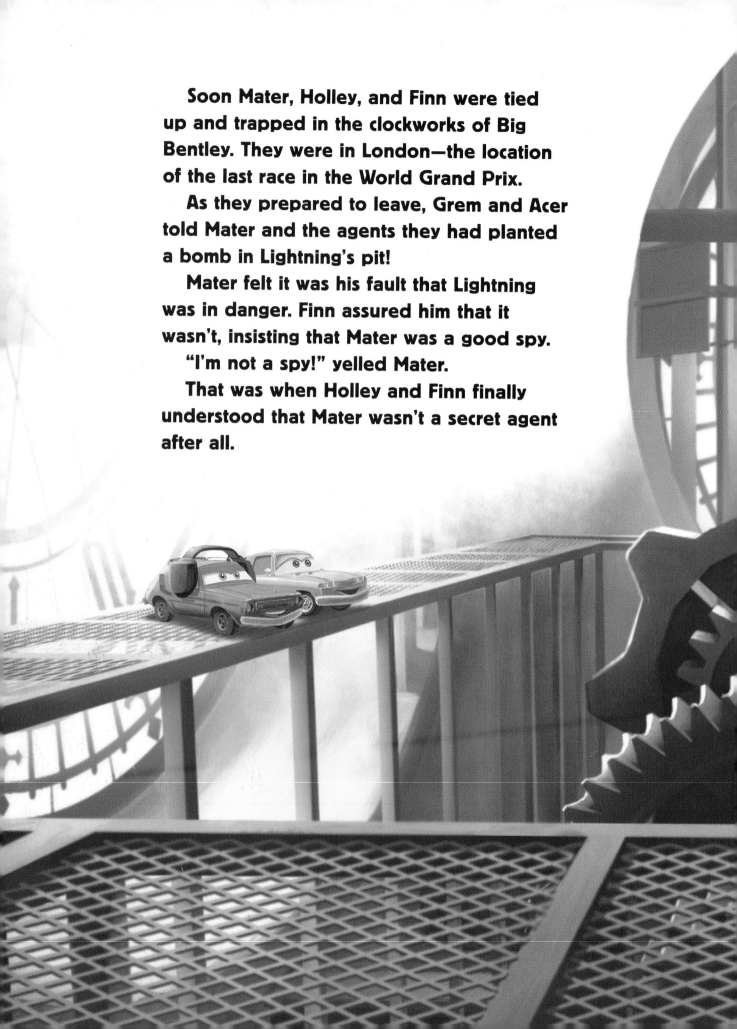

Soon Mater, Holley, and Finn were tied up and trapped in the clockworks of Big Bentley. They were in London—the location of the last race in the World Grand Prix.

As they prepared to leave, Grem and Acer told Mater and the agents they had planted a bomb in Lightning's pit!

Mater felt it was his fault that Lightning was in danger. Finn assured him that it wasn't, insisting that Mater was a good spy.

"I'm not a spy!" yelled Mater.

That was when Holley and Finn finally understood that Mater wasn't a secret agent after all.

As soon as Grem and Acer left, Mater used his spy gear to cut through his chains. He wanted to free Holley and Finn, but there was no time. He had to save Lightning!

Luckily, Holley and Finn were able to escape on their own.
They soon realized that Grem and Acer had actually planted
the bomb not in Lightning's pit, but on Mater! Finn sped
out of the clock tower while Holley extended her wings and
rocketed away!

Meanwhile, Mater arrived in the pits and saw everyone
from Radiator Springs. They had all come to help find him.
Lightning was so happy to see his best friend!
Suddenly, Finn called Mater and told him about the bomb.

Mater tried to race off to a safe distance. But Lightning wasn't going to let his best friend get away again. He hooked himself onto the tow truck, and the two friends blasted down the streets of London.

Grem and Acer were in hot pursuit! But Holley came to the rescue. She rammed into the Lemons and sent them flying into the air!

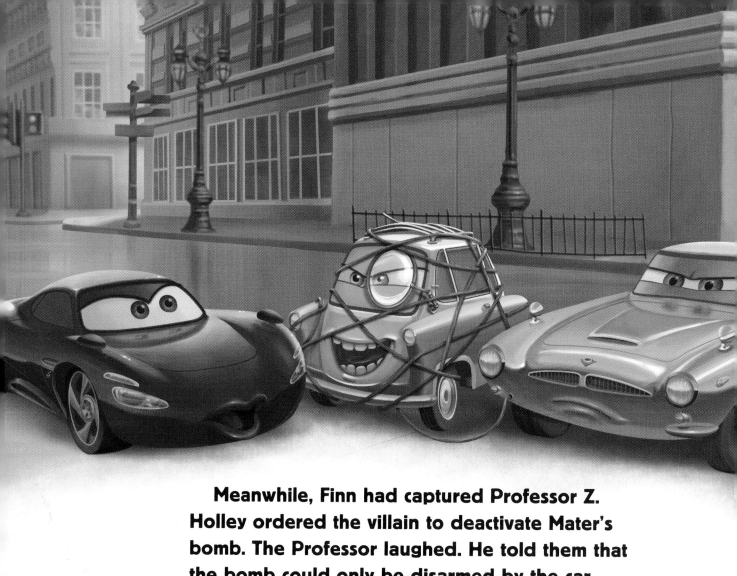

Meanwhile, Finn had captured Professor Z. Holley ordered the villain to deactivate Mater's bomb. The Professor laughed. He told them that the bomb could only be disarmed by the car who had activated it—the Lemons' Big Boss.

Suddenly, armies of Lemons arrived! But they were stopped by the Radiator Springs gang.

Guido, Ramone, Red, and Sheriff used all their tricks to defeat the Lemons.

When the battle was over, Mater figured out who the Big Boss was! Mater and Lightning took off for Buckingham Palace to tell the Queen.

When they arrived, the guards and even Finn blocked their way. They wouldn't let Mater get near the Queen with the ticking time bomb still attached. Lightning told Mater to start talking—fast!

Mater turned to Axlerod. "It's him!" he said. Mater explained that Axlerod had purposely made Allinol look unsafe so that cars would buy regular fuel again. Then Axlerod and his fellow Lemons would get rich selling the oil from their derrick.

Axlerod had no choice but to deactivate the bomb. Everyone was saved—and Mater was a hero!

At a special ceremony,
the Queen made Mater
a knight. His friends,
especially Lightning, were
very proud of him!

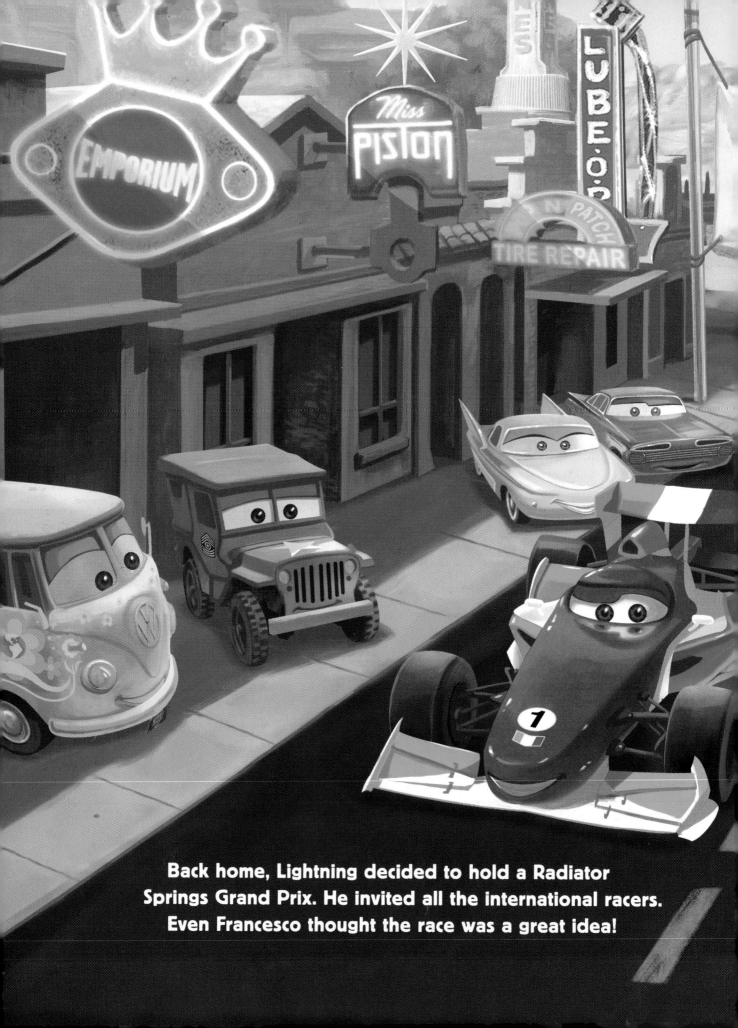

Back home, Lightning decided to hold a Radiator Springs Grand Prix. He invited all the international racers. Even Francesco thought the race was a great idea!

Mater was cheering Lightning on when Holley and Finn showed up. They wanted Mater to help them with their next mission.

Mater declined. He said he belonged with his best buddy in Radiator Springs.

But Mater did use his spy rockets one last time. Racing with Lightning was a blast!